A candy catastrophe!

"What's going on, Katie?" Nancy asked as they walked over.

"It's awful!" Katie said. "The jelly-bean jar for the contest is missing!"

Missing?

Nancy turned to look for the jelly-bean jar. The table it had been standing on yesterday was empty—except for the starry cardboard box!

"Mr. McCormick said that when he opened the store this morning the jar was already gone," Katie explained.

"I'm sorry, kids!" Mr. McCormick was saying. "But if the jelly-bean thief doesn't come forward by tomorrow afternoon, the contest will be called off!"

"Called off?" Nancy gasped. She looked at Bess and George. "It can't be!"

The Nancy Drew Notebooks

Available from Simon & Schuster

THE
NANCY DREW
NOTEBOOKS®

#61

Space Case

CAROLYN KEENE
ILLUSTRATED BY JAN NAIMO JONES

Aladdin Paperbacks
New York   London   Toronto   Sydney

First Aladdin Paperbacks edition August 2004
Copyright © 2004 by Simon & Schuster, Inc.

ALADDIN PAPERBACKS
An imprint of Simon & Schuster
Children's Publishing Division
1230 Avenue of the Americas
New York, NY 10020

The text of this book was set in Excelsior.

Printed in the United States of America
10 9 8 7 6 5 4 3 2 1

Library of Congress Control Number 2003114515

ISBN 0-689-86536-8

Space Case

1

Eye Spy

Go ahead, Bess," eight-year-old Nancy Drew said. "Pick a star and make a wish!"

It was Monday night. Nancy brushed her reddish-blonde bangs away from her eyes and stepped out of Bess's way. Bess tilted the telescope out Nancy's bedroom window toward the sky.

"What should I wish for?" Bess asked.

"How about a new bike? How about ice cream for dessert every day?" Nancy said to her best friend.

Nancy's other best friend, George Fayne, stood on her head against the wall. "I know!" she said. "Make a wish that you'll

win the Guess-the-Jelly-Beans contest!"

"Good idea!" Nancy said.

Earlier that day Nancy, Bess, and George had gone to McCormick's Supermarket to guess the number of jelly beans in a big glass jar. The boy or girl who guessed the closest would win a week at Cosmic Kids Space Camp!

Nancy, Bess, and George had studied the jelly beans in the jar. Then they each wrote their guess on a card and dropped it into a cardboard box decorated with stars.

Nancy loved guessing games. Guessing was like solving a mystery. And Nancy was the best detective at Carl Sandberg Elementary School!

"Starlight, star bright," Bess wished out loud. "I wish that George or Nancy wins the jelly bean contest."

"How come you didn't wish for yourself to win, Bess?" Nancy asked.

"I don't want to win!" Bess declared.

Nancy was surprised. She thought everybody wanted to win. "Why not, Bess?" she asked.

"I'm afraid of heights and aliens!" Bess

explained. "How can I go to space camp if I'm afraid of heights and aliens?"

George's dark curls bounced as she flipped over and landed on her back. Bess and George were cousins, but they didn't look alike or act alike.

"Give me a break, Bess!" George groaned. "The winner wins a week at space *camp*. It's where kids learn what it's like to be an astronaut!"

"*And* the winner gets to take along two friends," Nancy said. "So if one of us wins, we *all* get to go!"

Bess twirled her blonde ponytail between her fingers as she thought. She smiled and said, "Then I do wish we win!"

"I wish we knew exactly how many jelly beans were in that jar!" George said.

"Only Mr. McCormick knows for sure," Nancy reminded her. "He said he secretly filled the jar with tropical-flavored jelly beans from his store."

George giggled. "At least they weren't Smelly Jellies!" she said.

"Smelly Jellies!" Bess squealed.

"Ewww!" Nancy cried.

Smelly Jellies were the yuckiest jelly beans. They came in flavors like boiled egg, sardine, and sour milk!

"My turn!" George said. Bess stepped aside and George stood behind the telescope.

"What do you see?" Bess asked as George looked through the silver tube.

"Little green Martians!" George said. "And they're waving to us!"

"Martians?" Bess shrieked.

"Just kidding!" George laughed.

"Look for the Big Dipper," Nancy told George. "It's a bunch of stars that look like a pot with a handle."

George wasn't looking at the sky anymore. She was pointing the telescope straight out the window, toward the neighbors' houses.

"Hey!" George exclaimed. "I can see into other houses with this thing."

Nancy gasped. George was *snooping*! "George, it's not nice to snoop!" she scolded.

"I know," George admitted. "But I think I can see into Mike Minelli's house."

Mike lived a couple blocks away from

Nancy. He and his friends, Jason Hutchings and David Berger, were in the girls' third grade class. They were also major *pests*!

"What's Mike doing now?" Bess asked.

"Jason and David are in his room," George said. "They look like they're making piles of stuff on Mike's bed."

"What stuff?" Nancy asked.

"They look like . . . like . . ." George squinted her other eye. "Jelly beans!"

"Jelly beans?" Bess asked.

"Let me see." Nancy looked through the telescope. The boys *were* making tiny piles of jelly beans. "What are they doing with all those jelly beans?"

"The boys were at the supermarket today," Bess said. "Maybe they saw the jelly-bean jar and got hungry for some."

"Some?" George cried. "It looks like they've got *hundreds* of jelly beans."

Nancy wasn't sure why the boys had all those jelly beans. But she *was* sure of one thing: It wasn't nice to snoop!

"Let's look at the stars, not people," Nancy suggested. "That's why my dad put the telescope in my room."

"Yeah," Bess agreed. "And who wants to look at the boys anyway?"

Bess stood behind the telescope and tilted it toward the sky.

"Wowee, zowee!" she said. "How many stars do you think are in the sky, Nancy?"

Nancy gazed out the window. There seemed to be a million stars twinkling in the night sky. Maybe even a gazillion!

"All I know is this," Nancy said. "There are a lot more stars in the sky than all the jelly beans in the world!"

Tuesday morning Nancy woke up and glanced at her clock. It was 8:30 A.M. She usually woke up at seven-thirty when she had to go to school. But it was the middle of July and the middle of summer vacation!

Nancy washed up and got dressed, putting on her red shorts, white T-shirt, and sneakers. She ran downstairs to the kitchen. Her dad had already gone to work. Hannah was placing a fresh plate of muffins on the table.

Hannah Gruen was the Drews' housekeeper. She had been living with them since Nancy was three years old.

"Okay, guessing champ," Hannah said. "How many blueberries are in your muffin?"

Nancy studied the muffin on her plate. "Hmm," she said. "How about ten?"

"There's only one way to find out," Hannah said with a smile. "Eat it!"

The muffin was yummy. And Nancy counted nine blueberries. Pretty close!

After breakfast Hannah gave Nancy permission to buy a box of her favorite Popsicle at McCormick's Supermarket. Nancy called Bess and George to join her. They planned to meet at 10:00 A.M. on Main Street.

"The contest is still going on," Nancy said as they walked into McCormick's. "More kids probably came to guess today."

The first person Nancy saw in the supermarket was a woman wheeling a shopping cart. Her shiny brown hair was tied in the back with a white bow. She was wearing a sleeveless yellow dress and white sandals.

"Hello, girls," the woman said softly.

"Today I'm making photo albums out of bread slices. Won't that be fun?"

The woman smiled and wheeled her cart to the bread shelf.

"Isn't that Crafty Cathy?" George whispered. "The lady on TV who makes stuff out of food?"

Nancy thought the woman looked familiar! "Hannah watches Cathy's show all the time," she said. "Once she made a ring-toss game out of stale doughnuts."

Bess shook her head. "Doesn't Cathy ever *eat* the food?" she asked.

The girls walked through the supermarket. Nancy saw a bunch of kids gathered around Mr. McCormick. Their friend Katie Zaleski was there. Katie's parrot, Lester, was perched on her shoulder.

The kids looked worried.

"What's going on, Katie?" Nancy asked as they walked over.

"It's awful!" Katie said. "The jelly-bean jar for the contest is missing!"

Missing?

Nancy turned to look for the jelly-bean

jar. The table it had been standing on yesterday was empty—except for the starry cardboard box!

"Mr. McCormick said that when he opened the store this morning the jar was already gone," Katie explained.

"A goner! A goner!" Lester screeched. "Arrrk!"

Nancy, Bess, and George squeezed through the crowd to Mr. McCormick. He was wearing a white smock—and a big frown.

"I'm sorry, kids!" Mr. McCormick was saying. "But if the jelly-bean thief doesn't come forward by tomorrow afternoon, the contest will be called off!"

"Called off?" Nancy gasped. She looked at Bess and George. "It can't be!"

2
Thrills . . . and Chills!

But I *have* to go to space camp!" Orson Wong cried. "I've been practicing eating freeze-dried astronaut food for a week!"

"My father bought me a junior space suit for camp!" Brenda Carlton complained. "And a whole set of antigravity tennis balls!"

Orson and Brenda were also in Nancy's third-grade class. Orson could be a little pesty sometimes. And Brenda could be a little nasty *lots* of the time!

"There's nothing I can do, kids." Mr. McCormick said. Then he walked away.

"Great." Katie groaned. "If I won, I was going to take Lester to space camp. So he could be the first parrot in space!" Katie heaved a sad sigh. Then she carried Lester out of the store.

Nancy couldn't imagine who would steal the jelly beans. . . . Until she remembered what she saw through her telescope last night. She waved Bess and George over to the side.

"The boys had all those jelly beans in Mike's room. Remember?" Nancy whispered.

"Yeah!" George said. "And it looked like they were counting them, too!"

Nancy nodded. "Maybe the boys stole the jar so they could count the jelly beans and win the contest," she said.

"How could they sneak such a huge jar out of the store?" Bess asked.

Just then a teenage boy walked by. He was wearing the same white smock that everybody who worked at the supermarket had to wear.

"Hey," Nancy whispered. "Doesn't Mike Minelli have a cousin who works here?"

Bess nodded. "I think his name is Freddy . . . or Teddy—"

"Eddie!" George cut in. "Mike's cousin's name is Eddie."

"Maybe Eddie stole the jar for the boys," Nancy said.

"That's it!" George said. "Let's find Mr. McCormick and tell him what we think!"

The girls started to run. But when Nancy remembered her telescope, she screeched to a stop!

"Wait!" Nancy said. "If we tell Mr. McCormick what we saw last night, he'll know we were snooping!"

"So?" George asked.

"So I'm a detective, not a snoop!" Nancy said. "Before we accuse the boys of stealing the jar, we need more clues."

"Clues?" Bess asked. She gave a little excited jump. "Does that mean you're solving another mystery, Nancy?"

Nancy nodded. "But let's keep what we know about the boys a secret for now."

The girls went back to the crowd of kids. They were still talking about the missing jelly-bean jar.

"We might as well forget about the contest," Orson told the others. "We'll never know who stole the jelly-bean jar."

Bess stuck out her chin. "Yes, we will," she said. "Nancy *already* knows who stole the jelly beans!"

"Bess!" George hissed. "You weren't supposed to tell!"

Bess clapped her hand over her mouth. But it was too late. The kids were already surrounding Nancy!

"Who did it, Nancy?" Brenda demanded.

"I don't know for sure," Nancy insisted. "I need more clues."

"Clues, schmues!" Orson complained. "We want the thief and we want him now!"

Brenda stepped closer to Nancy. "If you *do* find the thief, Nancy," she said, "I'll write in my newspaper that you saved the Guess-the-Jelly-Beans contest."

Nancy knew all about Brenda's newspaper. It was called the *Carlton News*. She wrote it with her computer every month.

"What if I *don't* find the thief, Brenda?" Nancy asked.

Brenda shrugged. "Then I'll write that

you let down all the kids in River Heights," she said.

Brenda flipped her long hair. The other kids smiled at Nancy as they followed Brenda out of the supermarket.

"Great," Nancy muttered. "Now I really have to solve this case. Or else!"

Nancy pulled her blue detective notebook from her waist pack. Nancy carried it wherever she went so that she could write down all the suspects and clues of a mystery she was solving.

The girls started by searching around the table where the jar was last seen. The first things Nancy found were black marks on the floor. They looked like tire tracks.

"Maybe the thief wheeled the jelly-bean jar away," Nancy decided.

She opened her notebook. On a fresh page she wrote, "wheel tracks." On the next page she drew a partial map of the store.

"The table is right next to the candy shelf," Nancy said as she drew. "And very near the doors."

"Nancy!" George whispered. "There's Mike's cousin Eddie!"

Nancy looked up. A teenage boy with dark hair was wheeling a cart to the back of the store. It was filled with boxes. He wore a thick parka and blue jeans.

"How do you know that boy is Eddie?" Nancy whispered.

George cupped her hands around her mouth. "Hey, Eddie!" she shouted at the boy. "Where are the frozen pizzas?"

"Aisle five!" the boy shouted back.

George smiled. "Does that answer your question?" she asked.

Eddie stopped to unload his cart. Nancy wondered, *Did Eddie use the cart to wheel away the jelly-bean jar?*

"Why is Eddie bundled up like that?" Bess asked. "It's the summer!"

"Maybe he works in the freezer room," Nancy said. "It's always cold in there."

"Then we should check out the freezer room," George said. "If Eddie works there, he might have left some clues."

"No way am I going inside the freezer!" Bess said. "It's too cold in there!"

"Okay," George said with a shrug. "But

I'll bet that's where Mr. McCormick keeps all the ice cream and Popsicles."

"Ice cream? Popsicles?" Bess asked with wide eyes. She smiled and said, "Let's go!"

The girls ran to the freezer room at the back of the supermarket. First they made sure no one was looking. Then Nancy turned the handle on the big steel door. The door was heavy, but it swung open.

"Brr!" Nancy said as they stepped inside. "It's colder than I thought!"

"And I don't see any ice cream or Popsicles either!" Bess said.

"Forget the ice-cream and Popsicles," George said with a shiver. "Let's look for clues before we turn into kid-sicles!"

Nancy could see her cloudy breath as they searched the room. There were shiny steel freezers against the walls. In the middle of the room was a long table.

A white smock lay across the table. The name Eddie was stitched on the pocket.

"Eddie's smock!" Nancy said. She picked it up. A small piece of paper fell out of the pocket.

"Maybe it's a clue," Nancy said, picking it up. But when she tried to read it she frowned. "It's written backward!"

"Now we'll never know what it says," Bess said through chattering teeth.

"Yes, we will," George said. "I saw a trick in a detective movie once. All we have to do is hold the note up to a mirror, and the words will appear the right way!"

There were no mirrors around, so Nancy held the note up to a shiny freezer. Looking at the reflection, she read it out loud: "Eddie, thanks for the jelly beans. From Mike, Jason, and David."

"Ohmigosh!" Bess cried.

"Eddie *did* get the jelly beans for the boys!" George exclaimed.

Nancy heard a noise outside the freezer room. She shoved the note back into the smock. "Let's get out of here," she said. "Before Eddie gets back."

The girls raced to the door. Nancy pushed the handle down. This time the heavy door didn't open!

"Give it a push!" George said.

Nancy, Bess, and George pushed as hard

as they could on the door. But it didn't even budge.

Nancy's teeth began to chatter. She felt colder than she'd ever felt on the coldest winter day.

"I h-h-hate to say it," Nancy stammered. "But I th-think we're t-t-trapped!"

3

Spilling the Beans

Trapped?" Bess cried. She had goosebumps all over her arms and legs. George's lips were turning blue!

"Maybe Eddie locked us in here," George said, rubbing her arms. "As some kind of warning to us!"

"What are we going to do now?" Bess asked, jumping up and down.

"There's only one thing to do," Nancy said. She pounded on the door and shouted, "Heeeelp!!"

Nancy, Bess, and George all pounded on the door. Suddenly it swung wide open and they flew outside!

"Hey!" a voice demanded. "What were you girls doing in there?"

Nancy whirled around. Holding the freezer door open was Eddie Minelli!

"We were looking for the jelly-bean jar!" Nancy said, her teeth still chattering. "What do you know about it?"

Eddie smirked. "I know that it's missing," he said with a chuckle.

Nancy was about to ask Eddie about the note when Mr. McCormick called, "Eddie! This customer wants those frozen flounders!"

"Okay, Mr. McCormick!" Eddie called back. He looked at the girls and said, "And don't go back in there. The door sometimes freezes shut."

"Now he tells us," George muttered.

Nancy watched as Eddie walked into the freezer room and shut the door.

"The note was a great clue," Nancy said. "Now we know that Eddie got jelly beans for the boys."

"And he probably ate all the ice cream in the freezer room, too," Bess said.

Still shivering, Nancy, Bess, and George left the supermarket.

"Didn't you want to buy a box of Popsicles, Nancy?" Bess asked.

"Are you kidding?" Nancy cried. "After being in that freezer, all I want is hot chocolate."

The summer sun felt great. The girls went to the park to discuss the case. Nancy saw their friends Molly Angelo and Amara Shane. They were just leaving the playground with their jump ropes.

"Brenda told us about the missing jelly-bean jar, Nancy," Molly called. "We know you'll find it!"

"Good luck, Nancy!" Amara called. "We're all counting on you."

"I know, I know." Nancy sighed.

The girls sat down on a bench. Nancy opened her notebook to a fresh page. Then she wrote, "Things We Know About the Missing Jelly-Bean Jar."

"The jar was made out of glass," George said. "I know because I tapped on it when I tried to count the jelly beans."

"Mr. McCormick said the jelly beans inside were the tropical kind," Bess said.

"Like coconut, banana, and pineapple."

Nancy wrote the facts in her notebook. She turned the page and wrote,

Reasons We Think the Boys Stole the Jelly Beans
1) They had tons of jelly beans.
2) They wrote Eddie a note.
3) They're all major pests!

"Don't look now, Nancy," George whispered, "but look who's in the playground."

"George!" Nancy complained. "How can I look and *not* look at the same time?"

George pointed toward the playground. Nancy saw Jason, David, and Mike. They were chasing one another around the slide.

"Let's see what the boys are up to," Nancy whispered. She shut her notebook. The girls quietly ran behind a big tree.

Nancy peeked out from behind the tree. The boys were practicing karate kicks and hand chops. Suddenly Jason stopped and called out, "Jelly-bean break!"

Jelly-bean break? Nancy's heart skipped a beat. The boys reached into their pockets and pulled out handfuls of colorful jelly beans!

"Eat as many as you want!" Mike told his friends. "There's a lot more where those came from. A whole *jar* full!"

"Did you hear what he said?" Nancy whispered. "They have a *jar* of jelly beans!"

"And they're eating the evidence!" George said. "I'm stopping them now!"

"No!" Nancy warned. "First we have to make sure the boys are eating *tropical* jelly beans. Just like the stolen ones!"

"How?" Bess asked. "The boys will never share their jelly beans with us."

Jason and Mike finished their jelly beans. David stuffed the rest of his jelly beans in the pocket of his T-shirt.

"Follow me!" George whispered.

The girls stepped out from behind the tree. They began walking toward the boys.

"Jason, David, Mike!" George called. "Did you enter the space-camp contest?"

"Yeah, we did," David called back. "And we're going to win, too!"

Why are they so sure they're going to win? Nancy wondered.

"Well, you'd probably make horrible astronauts," George told the boys.

"Oh, yeah?" Mike asked.

"How come?" Jason demanded.

"There's no gravity in space," George explained. "Sometimes astronauts have to hang upside down for a long time. Bet you guys can't do that."

The boys looked at one another. Then Jason said, "Bet you we can!"

Jason, David, and Mike ran to the monkey bars. They climbed halfway up, grabbed the bars, and flipped upside down.

"See?" Jason called.

"Three . . . two . . . one," George counted down. Suddenly a shower of jelly beans poured out of David's pocket.

"Grab them!" George shouted.

Nancy smiled. So *that* was George's plan for getting the jelly beans!

The girls raced under the monkey bars and scooped up the jelly beans.

"Hey!" David shouted upside down. "Those are mine!"

"Finders, keepers, losers, weepers!" Bess said.

The girls held the jelly beans as they ran away from the playground.

"Some astronauts the boys would make," Nancy said as they ran. "They can't even get down from the monkey bars!"

Nancy, Bess, and George found a water fountain. They rinsed off the jelly beans.

"Let's do a taste test," Nancy said. "To see if the jelly beans are tropical."

Each of the girls popped a jelly bean into her mouth. But as Nancy chewed she didn't taste pineapple. Or banana. Or coconut.

"Sour milk!" Nancy gagged.

"Raw liver!" George sputtered.

"Rotten egg!" Bess cried.

Nancy shuddered as the jelly bean slid down her throat.

"These aren't tropical jelly beans," she cried. "They're *Smelly Jellies*!"

4

Snooper Blooper

"Yuck!" George sputtered. "And I thought licorice jelly beans tasted bad."

Bess frowned as George spit her jelly bean on the ground. "Ewww, George!" she scolded. "That is so gross."

"So are the jelly beans!" George said.

Nancy tossed the rest of her Smelly Jellies in the trash can. So did Bess and George. Then they raced back to the water fountain to rinse their mouths.

"Those couldn't be the stolen jelly beans," Nancy said. "Mr. McCormick didn't fill the jar with Smelly Jellies."

"Then what about the note the boys

wrote to Eddie?" George asked.

"And the jar the boys said they had," Bess added.

Nancy didn't get it either. But she decided to be fair. She turned to a clean page in her notebook and wrote,

Reasons We Think the Boys Didn't Steal the Jelly Beans
1) The jelly beans were Smelly Jellies.

"We'll see which page fills up first," Nancy said. "And then we'll know if the boys are guilty or not."

The girls started walking out of the park. Nancy could still taste sour milk on her tongue.

"Maybe we should look for the glass jar next," George suggested. "That's missing too."

Nancy looked at her watch and shook her head. "Can't," she said. "I have to go home and walk Chocolate Chip."

Chocolate Chip was Nancy's chocolate Labrador puppy. She walked him every day.

"I promised my mother I'd help her cook dinner," Bess said.

"That sounds like fun," Nancy said. "What are you eating for dinner, Bess?"

"Who knows?" Bess scrunched up her nose. "As long as it's not sour milk, raw liver, or rotten eggs!"

The girls made plans to meet the next morning. Time was running out. They had to solve the case before Mr. McCormick called off the contest the next afternoon.

By the time Nancy got home, Chip was happy to see her. She hooked on Chip's leash and walked her out of the house. The frisky puppy tugged at the lead until they were two blocks away from Nancy's house—on Mike Minelli's block!

"Let's go back, Chip," Nancy said. But when she looked at Mike's house, she saw something on his windowsill. It was round. And clear like glass.

It looks like a big jar, Nancy thought. *But it's too far away for me to be sure.*

Nancy didn't want to walk across Mike's yard.

"Maybe if I look at it through my tele-scope," Nancy thought out loud.

Chip barked at Nancy.

"You're right, Chip!" Nancy said. "It's not nice to snoop!"

Nancy walked Chip all the way home. She was happy to find her dad in the back-yard. He had come home from work early to barbecue dinner.

While Mr. Drew fired up the grill, Nancy helped Hannah set the picnic table.

"Hannah?" Nancy asked. "What are these greenish things under the plates?"

"They're place mats made out of cabbage leaves!" Hannah said. "Crafty Cathy made some on her show last week."

"Crafty Cathy?" Nancy asked. "I saw her at McCormick's Supermarket today!"

Hannah smiled. "Crafty Cathy thinks of everything, doesn't she?"

When Nancy was finished, she walked over to her dad. Mr. Drew was a lawyer and often helped Nancy with her cases. Today Nancy had an important question for him.

"Daddy, is it okay for detectives to

snoop?" Nancy asked. "You know, to use binoculars, tape recorders, telescopes?"

Mr. Drew turned a chicken drumstick on the grill. He wore a red apron with the words, "Now We're Cookin'" written on it.

"Why, Nancy?" Mr. Drew asked. "Did you see something through your telescope?"

"I think I saw something fishy," Nancy said slowly. "But I'm not sure."

Mr. Drew shook his head. "Snooping isn't a good idea, Nancy," he said. "What you see isn't always what you think you see."

"Really?" Nancy asked.

"Really," Mr. Drew said. He gave a little wink. "Stick to stargazing, Pudding Pie. Not people-gazing!"

Chip padded over to beg for some chicken. Nancy gently led her dog away by her collar.

Daddy's right, Nancy thought. *And I'm finding lots of evidence without my telescope anyway!*

Nancy ate a yummy dinner of barbecued chicken, potato salad, and cole slaw. When the sky got dark, Nancy went to her bedroom to look through her telescope.

"I will not snoop," Nancy told herself. "I will not snoop."

Chip sat at Nancy's feet as she tilted the telescope out her window. She pressed one eye against the eyepiece and looked through. The stars seemed extra-bright tonight.

"I heard there's something called the Dog Star, Chip!" Nancy said. "I wonder if it's shaped like a dog, too."

"Woof!" Chip barked. She tried to jump on Nancy's lap. The telescope tilted down straight toward Mike's room!

"Down, Chip!" Nancy scolded. She was about to tilt up the telescope when she saw something through the lens. It was the round, clean thing she'd seen on Mike's windowsill before.

Nancy stared at it.

Through the telescope it *really* looked like a jar. It looked about the same size and shape as the one missing from McCormick's Supermarket!

"Ohmigosh!" Nancy gasped. "Could that be the missing jelly-bean jar?"

5

Jar Too Far

Chip nuzzled her nose against Nancy's elbow.

"I know I'm snooping, Chip," Nancy said. "But I've got to get a better look at that jar!"

Nancy twisted the knob on her telescope that made things look closer. Was the jar made out of glass? How could she tell?

Suddenly Mike came to the window—and pulled down the shade. The jar was out of sight!

"Phooey!" Nancy muttered. She leaned back in her chair. "But at least I have a great new clue, right, Chip?"

Chip wagged her tail.

Nancy grabbed her notebook. She turned to "Reasons We Think the Boys Stole the Jelly Beans" and added a fourth reason: "Mike has a jar on his windowsill."

"And tomorrow I'm going to find out if it's the *missing* jar!" Nancy declared.

"Is that the jar you were talking about, Nancy?" George said. "The one in the window?"

It was Wednesday morning. Nancy, Bess, and George rode their bikes to Mike's block. They stood on the sidewalk and stared at Mike's window. The shade was up. The jar was still on the windowsill.

"That's it," Nancy said.

"It's the same shape as the missing jelly-bean jar," Bess said. "And I'll bet it's the same size, too!"

"What else can it be? It *has* to be the missing jelly-bean jar!" George asked.

"We don't know for sure," Nancy said. "We have to get a closer look."

"Cool," George said. "Let's look through your telescope!"

"No!" Nancy said. "Last night's snooping was an accident. There has to be another way we can get a closer look."

"Snooping! Snooping!" a voice cried out. "Arrrk!"

Nancy turned around and smiled. It was Katie's parrot, Lester. He was sitting on Katie's shoulder as he usually did.

"What's going on?" Katie asked. She walked over to the girls. "Why were you guys talking about snooping?"

Nancy didn't want to tell everyone what she'd seen through her telescope. But Katie was her friend. So Nancy told her about the telescope and what she'd seen.

"Please solve the case and save the contest, Nancy," Katie said. "I have to take Lester to space camp!"

"Whoever heard of a parrot at space camp?" George asked.

Katie shrugged. "There was a dog in outer space," she said. "And a chimpanzee. Why can't a parrot be an astronaut too?"

Nancy couldn't picture Lester in space. Would he wear a teeny, tiny spacesuit? Or eat freeze-dried crackers?

"How do you know Lester wants to go to outer space, Katie?" Nancy asked.

Lester blinked. "Mission control! Mission control!" he screeched. "Arrrk!"

Katie smiled her biggest smile. "That's how!" she said.

Nancy turned toward Mike's house. "Come on," she said. "We have to get closer to that window."

The girls inched across Mike's yard. Soon they were standing underneath Mike's window and the jar.

"Look!" Bess said, pointing up. "The jar has some jelly beans on the bottom."

"I'll bet they're Smelly Jellies," Nancy said.

"The green ones are probably pickle flavored," George said. "And the yellow ones are probably sauerkraut!"

"I'll bet the white ones are turnip flavored," Bess added. "Or maybe they taste like cauliflower—"

Lester flapped his feathery wings. He began squawking, "Eat 'em up! Arrrk!"

Nancy gasped as Lester flew right up to Mike's window!

"Lester—come back!" Katie called.

Lester landed on Mike's windowsill. He began pecking at the side of the jar!

"What's he doing?" Nancy asked.

"I guess he's trying to get to the Smelly Jellies," Katie said.

"Why?" George cried.

"Parrots love vegetables," Katie explained. "And most of the Smelly Jellies are veggie flavored."

"Chow down!" Lester screeched from Mike's windowsill. "Raaaak!"

"Oh, great!" Nancy groaned. "What if Mike is somewhere in the house? What if he finds Lester in his room?"

Lester stretched his neck to reach into the jar. It toppled back and forth!

"Oh no!" Bess cried. "Lester is going to knock the jar down!"

Katie cupped her hands around her mouth. "Lester!" she yelled. "Step away from the jar. Step away from the jar!"

"Oooh, boy!" Lester screeched. He gave a little jump, and the jar tipped over the windowsill!

"Get back!" George shouted, waving her arms. "It's going to crash!"

The girls scattered in four directions as the jar fell from the window. Nancy squeezed her eyes shut as it landed on the cement path. But she didn't hear it crash. Or smash.

Nancy opened her eyes. The jar had bounced on the ground and rolled to a stop.

"You guys," Nancy said slowly, "I have a funny feeling that's *not* the missing jelly-bean jar."

6

Clue Out of the Blue

H ow can it not be the jar, Nancy?" Bess asked. "It looks just like it!"

"A glass jar would have smashed on the cement," Nancy explained. She knelt down and tapped the jar. "This one is made out of plastic."

Everyone was quiet as Nancy pulled out her detective notebook. She turned to her not-guilty page and added "Plastic jar" to the list.

"You mean the boys didn't steal the jelly-bean jar, Nancy?" Katie asked.

Nancy wasn't sure. How could the boys

seem guilty and innocent at the same time?

Suddenly she heard a loud "RAAACK!"

Everyone turned. Lester was zooming out of Mike's window!

"Get out and stay out, cracker breath!" Mike yelled. He was shaking his fist and was dressed in his *Moleheads from Mars* space suit. *Moleheads from Mars* was the boys' favorite TV show.

"He was eating the crackers on my bed!" Mike shouted out the window. "And he pecked my nose too! What are you doing here anyway?"

Nancy pointed to the few jelly beans that spilled out of the jar. "Where did you get the jelly beans, Mike?" she asked.

"My cousin Eddie bought them," Mike shouted. "They're Smelly Jellies!"

Eddie? That explained the note. But it didn't explain something else.

"Why did Eddie buy you all those Smelly Jellies?" Nancy asked.

"They're the cheapest jelly beans in the store," Mike explained. "Nobody likes them. Except my friends and me."

"We know that," Nancy said. "But you still didn't tell me why he bought them!"

"None of your business!"

Mike disappeared from the window. He reappeared with his *Moleheads from Mars* water blaster in his hands.

"Return to your planet at once, invaders!" Mike ordered in a deep voice.

The girls shrieked as he squirted a blast of cold water at them.

"Lester hates water!" Katie said as she hurried away. "We're out of here!"

Nancy, Bess, and George raced to their bikes and put on their helmets. The cold water didn't feel bad. But nobody wanted to deal with a pesty Molehead!

They pedaled until they were a few blocks away from the Minelli house.

"Are we going to look for more clues?" Bess asked. She twirled the pink streamers on her bicycle handle.

"We don't have time to look for more clues, Bess," George said. "Mr. McCormick said he'll call off the contest this afternoon if the thief isn't caught."

"Don't remind me." Nancy groaned.

"Now Brenda will write that I let everyone down. And she'll be right!"

"Who cares what Miss Snooty Pants writes?" George asked. "Let's find Mr. McCormick and ask him for more time."

"And let's not forget to say 'please,'" Bess added.

The girls rode straight to Main Street. Nancy saw a crowd of kids outside the supermarket. They looked even more disappointed than yesterday.

"What's up?" George called as they parked their bicycles at the curb.

Brenda narrowed her eyes at Nancy. She took one step to the side. Right behind her was a big sign that read:

SORRY, KIDS. JELLY-BEAN CONTEST
CANCELLED.

Nancy gulped. Mr. McCormick had already called off the contest.

"We thought you'd find the thief, Nancy!" Amara said.

"Yeah, Nancy!" Orson said. "You even said you were close!"

Bess stepped forward. "Nancy *was* close!" she said. "She thought she saw the thieves right through her own telescope!"

Nancy froze.

Bess clapped her hand over her mouth again. But it was too late.

"Telescope?" Brenda asked. "Does that mean you were *snooping*, Detective Drew?"

Everyone gasped.

Nancy didn't say a word. She knew Brenda would write about her telescope in the *Carlton News* no matter what she said.

"Come on," Nancy told Bess and George. "Let's find Mr. McCormick."

The girls still wore their bicycle helmets as they walked into the supermarket. They found Mr. McCormick by the fruit section. He was helping a customer pick out a ripe cantaloupe.

"Mr. McCormick?" Nancy asked. "We know you already cancelled the contest, but can you give us more time to find the thief? Please?"

"Sorry," Mr. McCormick said as he picked up a cantaloupe. "It wouldn't be fair if the thief counted the jelly beans."

"But, Mr. McCormick," Nancy started to say. "We think we can—"

"Hello, Mr. McCormick," a soft voice called out.

Nancy spun around. It was Crafty Cathy again—wheeling her cart up the same aisle.

"Today I'm making bookmarks out of dried banana peels," Cathy said.

Mr. McCormick pointed to the bananas. "Take as many bananas as you like, Cathy," he said. "They're on the house, as usual!"

Crafty Cathy smiled as she wheeled her cart to the bananas.

"On the house?" George asked. "You mean everything is free for Crafty Cathy?"

Mr. McCormick nodded. "Cathy mentions our store on her show every day," he said. "It's very good for business."

Nancy looked past Mr. McCormick at Crafty Cathy. She was wearing colorful earrings. And a colorful bracelet, too.

Nancy looked closer. The jewelry was not

made out of gems. Or stones. Or even beads. The earrings and bracelet were made out of—

"Jelly beans!" Nancy gasped.

Nancy quietly pointed them out to Bess and George.

"You don't think *Crafty Cathy* stole the jelly beans, do you?" Bess whispered.

Nancy quickly put the pieces together. "Cathy is always wheeling a cart," she whispered. "And she can take anything out of the store without paying for it."

Crafty Cathy spun her cart around. She began wheeling it away from the fruit.

"Let's stop her," Nancy told her friends. "We have to ask her questions!"

Crafty Cathy picked up speed as she wheeled her cart toward the exit. The girls ran after her. But when they sped around a corner, they ran right into a tower of cereal boxes! WHAM!! The girls shrieked as the cardboard boxes tumbled to the floor.

"Oh no!" Mr. McCormick wailed. "My Flakey Wakey Cereal tower is ruined!"

The girls helped to rebuild the Flakey

Wakey tower. When they were done, they ran outside. Crafty Cathy was gone!

"We have to find Crafty Cathy right away," Nancy declared. "I think she's the jelly-bean thief!"

7

Crafty Confession

Where do you think Crafty Cathy went?" Bess asked as they looked around.

"Maybe she went to the TV station," Nancy said. "Her show is on every day."

The girls hopped on their bicycles. They rode quickly and carefully down Main Street to the WRIV TV station.

After parking their bikes, they walked through the spinning doors. A guard was sitting behind a desk in the waiting room.

"Sorry, kids," he told them. "Mr. Lizard is on vacation this month."

Mr. Lizard's Playhouse was the girls' favorite television show. But they weren't at the station to see Mr. Lizard today.

"We'd like to speak to Crafty Cathy, please," Nancy said.

The guard looked surprised. "You kids watch Crafty Cathy?" he asked.

"Only once," Bess said. "When she stuffed pillows with cotton candy."

The guard picked up a telephone. "I'll let Cathy's producer know you're here," he said. "In the meantime you can watch the show on that monitor."

He pointed to a TV set at the side of the room. Crafty Cathy was on the screen.

"Thank you," Nancy said.

The girls sat on the floor in front of the set. George pointed to the screen.

"Look!" she said. "She's wearing the jelly-bean jewelry in the show."

Nancy wiggled toward the set for a closer look. It *was* the same jewelry she'd worn in the supermarket.

Crafty Cathy walked over to something that looked like an easel. A white cloth was draped over it.

"Today we're going to get jazzy with jelly beans," Crafty Cathy said. "Look what I made with just a jar full of jelly beans and a little imagination."

Cathy yanked off the cloth.

Underneath was a picture of Cathy. But it wasn't made of paint or colored pencils. It was made out of—

"Jelly beans!" Nancy cried.

"Hundreds of them!" Bess gasped.

"For my self-portrait I used tropical flavors," Crafty Cathy said. "And you can buy them at McCormick's Supermarket."

"Tropical flavors?" the girls shouted at the same time.

Nancy, Bess, and George jumped up. They stared at the television screen.

"That's proof enough for me!" George said. She pointed to the TV. "Crafty Cathy is guilty as charged!"

"Guilty of what?" a voice asked.

Nancy spun around. Standing right behind them was Crafty Cathy!

"W-w-we thought you were on TV!" Nancy stammered.

Crafty Cathy smiled. "My show was taped this morning," she said. "That's why I'm out here and not in the studio. So just what is it that I'm guilty of?" she demanded.

Nancy took a deep breath and asked, "Ms. Crafty? Did you take the big jelly-bean jar out of McCormick's Supermarket on Monday?"

"You can call me Cathy," Crafty Cathy said. "And I did put the jar in my cart. And wheeled it out of the store."

The girls' mouths dropped open. Not only did Crafty Cathy confess—she didn't seem to care!

"Why did you take the jelly-bean jar, Cathy?" Nancy asked.

Crafty Cathy shrugged. "I asked a check-out girl where the jelly beans were," she said. "The girl pointed toward the jar and told me to help myself."

Nancy waved Bess and George away from Crafty Cathy.

"I don't get it," Nancy whispered.

"Me neither," George whisperd. "Why would the girl tell Cathy to take the jelly beans from the contest?"

Nancy tried to picture the girl pointing to the jelly-bean jar.

"Hmm," Nancy said slowly. "What if the

girl didn't really point to the jar."

"What do you mean?" Bess asked.

Nancy lifted her notebook out of her waist pack. She turned to the map she'd drawn and studied it carefully.

"Look," Nancy said. She ran her finger along the map. "The jelly-bean jar was right between the candy shelf and the check-out counters."

"So?" George asked.

"What if the check-out girl meant to point to the candy shelf?" Nancy said.

Bess gasped. "Cathy could have thought the girl pointed to the jelly-bean jar instead!" she said.

Nancy explained everything to Crafty Cathy. She showed her the map, too.

"It was a mistake!" Crafty Cathy said. "I would never have taken those jelly beans if I knew the contest was still going on. I thought it was over!"

Nancy smiled. She believed Crafty Cathy. And was glad she wasn't a thief!

"I'll bring the jar back to the super-market later today," Cathy promised. "And explain everything to Mr. McCormick."

"Yes!" Bess cheered.

"Maybe Mr. McCormick will start the space-camp contest again!" George said.

"And," Crafty Cathy added, "since you are such good detectives, I'd like to give you each a little present."

Crafty Cathy reached into her pocket and pulled out three jelly-bean bracelets. She handed one to each of the girls!

"Wow!" Bess exclaimed. "We'll be the best-dressed girls at space camp!"

"*If* we win the contest," Nancy pointed out.

The girls dangled their colorful bracelets on their wrists. After thanking Crafty Cathy, they left the TV studio.

"These bracelets are way cool!" George said outside.

"I thought you didn't like bracelets, George," Bess said.

"I don't," George said. She licked her lips. "But I love jelly beans!"

Nancy, Bess, and George walked back to their bicycles.

"Aren't you happy, Nancy?" Bess asked. "You solved the case. And you saved the space-camp contest, too!"

Nancy *was* happy. But she still had one question. . . .

"If the boys didn't steal the jelly-bean jar," Nancy wondered, "then what were they doing with all those jelly beans?"

8

The Winner Is . . .

It's a party on Main Street!" Nancy said happily. "A space party!"

It was a whole week after Nancy solved the case. Almost all the kids in River Heights were on Main Street to find out the winner of the Guess-the-Jelly-Beans contest.

When Crafty Cathy brought back the empty jar, Mr. McCormick had filled it again with the same secret amount of jelly beans. And the contest was on!

"Wow!" George said. She gave a low whistle. "Look how many kids showed up!"

Nancy glanced around. Most of the kids in the crowd were dressed up as astronauts, aliens, and even rocket ships. Katie was there with Lester on her shoulder. She was wearing a T-shirt that read: LESTER, FIRST PARROT IN SPACE!

Nancy, Bess, and George wore pins shaped like stars and planets—and their jelly-bean bracelets, of course!

"Out of my way, out of my way!" a voice commanded.

Nancy turned to see Orson Wong spinning around in circles. His arms and legs were wrapped in silver foil. The cap on his head was made of silver foil too.

"What are you supposed to be?" George joked. "A baked potato?"

"Duh!" Orson said, spinning. "I'm a super satellite. And I'm orbiting Earth!"

Orson suddenly stopped. He grabbed his tummy and groaned.

"I think the super-satellite just got super-dizzy!" Bess whispered.

"Attention, kids!" Mr. McCormick called out. He stood on a stage built in front of the supermarket. On a small table was the jelly-bean jar. Standing next to him was a woman wearing a blue pantsuit.

"That's Janet Weston, a real-live astronaut!" Nancy said excitedly. "I once saw her picture in a kids magazine!"

"An astronaut?" Bess asked. "I wonder if *she's* afraid of heights or aliens."

"Speaking of aliens," George whispered, "here come the boys."

Jason, David, and Mike were wearing their *Moleheads from Mars* costumes as they pushed their way through the crowd.

"And now," Mr. McCormick called out, "it's time to find out who is the winner!"

Nancy stared at the jelly-bean jar. Was her guess close? Close enough to win?

"The winner of the Guess-the-Jelly-Beans contest is . . ." Mr. McCormick began to say.

Janet handed him a card. Nancy's heart beat faster as Mr. McCormick read the card to himself. Then he looked up and announced, "Mike Minelli."

Nancy's heart sank. She could hear Bess and George groan. Not only did they lose, they lost to one of the boys!

"We're going to space camp!" Mike yelled. "We're going to space camp!"

The three boys ran up onstage.

"Congratulations, Mike," Janet said. "Your guess was exactly right!"

"Exactly right?" Nancy gasped. If the boys didn't steal the jar, how did they know the exact number of jelly beans?"

"We *didn't* guess!" Mike told Janet. "We had the whole thing planned out!"

"What do you mean?" Janet asked.

"First we bought a jar the same size as the one in the contest," Jason said. "Then we filled it with as many Smelly Jellies as would fit inside."

"Next we counted all the jelly beans in the jar," David said.

"Then we ate them," Mike added. "The toe-jam flavor rocked!"

"Ewwww!" Bess cried.

Nancy stared at Bess and George. So that's what the boys were doing with all those jelly beans!

"What do you say, Ms. Weston?" Mike asked. "When do we blast off?"

"Not so fast, guys," Janet said. "This was supposed to be a guessing contest."

"So?" Mike asked.

"You didn't guess," Janet said firmly. "So you can't win."

"You mean we can't go to space camp?" David cried.

Mike pointed at his cousin Eddie in the crowd. "This was all your idea!" he shouted. "Thanks a lot, cement-head!"

Suddenly Nancy had a horrible thought. What if Mr. McCormick called off the contest again?

"Luckily we have a runner-up," Mr. McCormick said to the crowd. "The kid with the *next* closest guess is . . ."

He looked at a card. Then he looked at the crowd and said, "Nancy Drew!"

Bess and George shrieked. Nancy was too surprised to say anything. But she jumped up and down with her friends.

"You won, Nancy!" Bess cheered.

"You're going to space camp!" George cheered.

"*We're* going to space camp!" Nancy said. "And we're going to have a blast!"

Orson and Katie hurried over.

"Don't forget to pack astronaut food,"

Orson said. "The freeze-dried tacos are pretty good."

"And if you do go to space," Katie said, "don't forget to take Lester!"

Nancy saw Brenda squeeze through the crowd. She wore a junior astronaut suit and matching space helmet. In her hand was a copy of the *Carlton News*.

"Here." Brenda shoved the newspaper in Nancy's hand. "I wrote a whole article about you. It's on the first page."

Nancy's stomach did a triple-flip. Did Brenda write about her telescope? Did she call Nancy a snoop? But when Nancy looked at the front page she smiled. The headline read: NANCY DREW SAVES SPACE CAMP CONTEST!

"Thanks, Brenda!" Nancy said.

"A deal's a deal," Brenda said with a sigh.

"Now you have to write a new headline, Brenda," George said. "One that reads 'Nancy *wins* the space-camp contest'!"

Next came the most exiting part of all. The girls filed up onstage to meet Janet Weston.

"How did you do it, Nancy?" Janet asked. "Was it a lucky guess?"

Nancy thought so. Until she remembered a wish she made a few nights ago. "I think it was a lucky *star*, Ms. Weston," she said. "A very lucky star!"

That night Mr. Drew took Nancy, Bess, and George to a restaurant to celebrate. It was called Mission Control. The waiters were dressed like aliens and served dishes with names like Planetary Pizza and Galaxy Guacamole.

Nancy ordered Space-age Spaghetti with Meteor Meatballs. For dessert she had Astro Apple Pie.

"Do you think there are aliens in outer space?" Bess asked as she sipped her Martian Milkshake.

George ate a spoonful of her Stardust Sundae. "I don't know," she said. "But they sure can cook!"

Nancy felt great.

It was the perfect ending to a perfect day. But it wasn't over yet. . . .

When she got home, Nancy went up to

her room. This time she didn't go to her telescope. She went straight to her detective notebook and began to write. . . .

Daddy was right when he said snooping isn't a good idea. What you see isn't always true. But I *am* going to space camp, and that's the truth!

Maybe I'll even go to space someday. There must be mysteries up there, too. In the meantime I have the next best things: Cosmic Kids Space Camp and my telescope!

Case closed!